The
Dream and Drink
of
Freedom

Johnny Dolphin

Introduction by Kathelin Hoffman

SYNERGETIC PRESS

FIRST EDITION

Published by Synergetic Press, Inc.
Post Office Box 689, Oracle, Arizona 85623
24 Old Gloucester Street, London WC1 3AL

Cover design by Berthold Wolpe, with line drawing by Gerald Wilde. Page design by Kathleen Dyhr.

Typesetting by Synergetic Press on Studio Software

ISBN 0-907791-158

Printed in Great Britain by Express Litho Service (Oxford).

CONTENTS

INTRODUCTION

Dolphin was born and reared in the lingering traditions of the frontier. The Texan side of his family was killed in one of the great family feuds. One lone survivor, Dolphin's grandfather, moved to Oklahoma in the 1890's. At age five, Dolphin spent long summer days sitting in the back of a combine, bathing in a shower of golden wheat, or lying in cool muddy hog wallows. At age twelve he would accompany 'big handed men' who ate a 5 course breakfast before working 14 hours in the fields.

His grandfather died at 68 when he fell and hit his head during a fist fight with a young upstart government agent. The Oklahoma frontier died too; the dustbowl from its eroded plains was reported to be seen as far as Washington, D.C. Dolphin left home at 14 to join the wave of Okies heading to California. There he picked fruit in the inner valley, worked in a factory, and was befriended by refugee European intelligensia, playing chess with them on the palisade of Santa Monica on Sunday afternoons.

I first met Johnny Dolphin in 1967 at a bus stop in San Francisco's North Beach. He was six foot one, brawny, with Cherokee cheekbones that jutted like cliffs on a windswept face, a glance alternately musing and fierce, an everpresent dolphin's smile, a Jovial intellect that contemplated geologic epochs and calculated orders of magnitude. He was prone to quote the Persian poet Rumi and the great football coach Knute Rockne in the same breath.

Scattered impressions of the twenty succeeding years: Dolphin voraciously studying planetary maps at the U.S. Geologic Survey; tears of delight pouring down his cheeks while savoring sweet potato pie in Harlem; sharing cosmologies with shamans of the Amazon; furiously scribbling an outline for a space-travellers' civilisation on paper napkins in a Bowery diner; tromping

i

clods of the Hungarian plain beneath his boots seeking a glimpse of the great bustard ...

The Dream and Drink of Freedom is the second published volume of Dolphin's poetry. The first, which bore the same title, was published in Chicago in 1951. Over 500 copies were confiscated and burned by Savonarolas of the McCarthy period in 1952 while Dolphin was in the army and I have been unable to find a copy from this edition of 1000.

The present volume includes selected poems written between 1946 and 1986. These poems chronicle both a personal and social history of essence America where eternal vigilance is the price of liberty.

Part One (1946-48). "I must shape the God that I have seen" (from 'Dedication'). In crackling nature poems, the poet contemplates the big-spirited cycles of Great Nature. Dolphin knew these cycles intimately as a youth. His awe for them and discontent with man's failure to appreciate them became recurrent themes in his later poems.

Part Two (1949-54). "Plot of legalised rant/Mad hymn to the reddened sky/Defying forty miles of steel/ With voices, a box, a corner lamp--/O Free Speech Square" (from 'Washington Square, Chicago, USA'). In Chicago, Dolphin lived as a street poet and worked in the stockyards, holding the position of secretary of the UPWA-CIO District 10 anti-discrimination committee. He had the opportunity to meet W.E.B. duBois and Paul Robeson, whose insights on art and history highly influenced him. This section celebrates and investigates the postwar confidence of victorious working people heady with the New Deal.

Part Three (1955-60). "We go to graves on shields of metal dreams" (from 'Song Heard in Pittsburgh'). As a young engineer, Dolphin determinedly looked futureward. His dream of space travel first appears in 'Pallas Athene', 1957, inspired by the Sputnik launch. 'Conversation in Cambridge', 1961 reveals the inner contradictions he encountered in the Harvard enclave, where he was a Baker Scholar. As a metallurgist at

Allegheny-Ludlam, Dolphin sings of an America impassioned with pure matter and the raw power of industry ('Song of Pittsburgh', 'Metal'). In his memoirs, David Lilienthal called Dolphin "a bright young rolling stone ... a metallurgist by profession and a poet by inclination." [1] Working for Lilienthal in Manhattan, Dolphin revels in the day world of the corporate executive ('Wall Street, N.Y.') and in the bohemian night world ('Kiwi') as a poet roaming the artistic turf of the Village after dark.

Part Four (1961-66). "Shiva became restricted to six arms, ten forms and twenty-four incarnations" (from 'One Song of India'). Kennedy was shot, and with him, the aspirations of a generation. Dolphin abruptly left the U.S., determined to explore other cultures, and thereby to re-evaluate his own and reformulate his goals. Expatriate pilgrimages took Dolphin throughout Africa and Asia, culminating in war-torn Vietnam, where he alternated being a wandering Buddhist scholar and being a stringer doing the footwork for a correspondent ensconced in Saigon.

Part Five (1967-83) "How can I get it for you if you don't tell me what you want" (from 'Interzone'). Dolphin returned to the United States transformed by his experiences. He was determined to launch a unique personal future. Poems in this section come from his fertile playwriting years when Dolphin wrote over 35 plays. [2] At the same time, he began to travel annually around the planet, convinced that history had outgrown the nation state. He helped establish a series of major ecological projects and co-founded a theater company.

Part Six (1984-86). "Only the unpredictable/ ignites the dream" (from 'Message Found Engraved'). This last phase shows the poet at his prime, sipping the matured wine of his life, having attained his own individuality, contemplating man's place in the cosmos. Dense with the bustle of ideas and visions, these poems accompanied the formation of Space Biospheres Ventures, the revolutionary space-science project. The poems in this section integrate styles from his previous work. He takes a new theme, the investigation and realisation of impossibility.

Literary influences threading through Dolphin's poetry include the rousing ardor of Mayakovsky, the ecstatic wrath of Blake, celebratory eloquence of Whitman, the thick syntax of Joyce, the droll cut-ups of Burroughs, the terse apercu of Brecht's poems and the love of the unknown of Khayyam and Baudelaire.

A master of a variety of styles, all of Dolphin's work is characterised by restless, intense energy. His poems burst with crisp Apollonian architectonics, with seething images, fierce grunts, impetuous longing, and discontent.

Ginsberg in "Howl" sung the fate of the American poet. Dolphin seeks to define in words and action not the fate but the poet's destiny in the scientific age. His poet is an inner space traveller articulating humanity's dream of immortality. He writes, "In the ecology of man/poetry is the indicator species/of the health of the dream."

The word 'poet' means 'maker'. Dolphin adopts the 'magic if' of the dreamer whose life is his poem, who creates a world nearer to his heart's desire, an investigator of the impossible, a maker of new dreams and creator of new worlds.

Kathelin Hoffman
January, 1987

1 *The Journals of David E. Lilienthal,* Vol. VI, p. 94, Harper and Row.

2 See *Collected Works of Caravan of Dreams Theater,* Synergetic Press.

I

DEDICATION

I have run laughing in tiredness,
Thought shadows gaily dappled,
Swum carefree with sunburnt days,
Enjoyed the fragile love game.

Oh, watching flesh and grass
Shuttle cheap lovely fabrics
Over bone and rock,
I was dismayed by death
Until I centered search
Past fireflies in river groves,
Past girls bathing in summer,
Into wilder regions
Through dry thunder and lightning,
Towards the dark hang
Shrouding and swaddling cliffs --

Starswept from birth in plains
Of noon-hammered grain
Where full moons, bloodred,
Brood over Indian ghosts and bluestem --
Here out of superhighways of change,
From caravans more parti-colored than Judea's,
From jet trails and blinking neons
I must shape the God that I have seen.

HARVEST AND STUDY

O for the sweat, cursings, and weariness of harvest!
For the heaping plates of good coarse food
And the silent sleep under silent stars,
For the ripe golden grain and the meadowlark,
For the whole bursting plenty of earth producing,
For the rattle and clamor and roar of trucks and combines,
For the men, strong, smelling of sweat,
Men of obscenities and appetites, men of the plains.

DROUGHT

Crack, you river mud,
Creak, you waterless windmills.
Heat flashes lightning
Like sparks in a car out of gas.
The sand scours our lives,
We wear too fast for rust;
Bright and hard, without guilt,
We fight outraged soil's revenge.
We shoot silver iodide into clouds
And change the shape of plows.
Never, never shall we cry,
but bend our back and brain to task.
We will never cry,
We will not admit our guilt,
How can nature's drought scare us,
We who have dried the thought of tears?

AGAIN OCTOBER

Again October!

Beagles give cry at rabbits
Through toppled stalks of corn,
And boys unburdened with regrets
Find fires in frost of dawn.

And thoughtless lovers pause,
Then tighten each to each,
Against both Change and Cause,
Their hope turned frail as touch.

And fingerlike the sun
Twines around trees
As if a huntsman home
Mulling ale-foamed lees.

IN AN OKLAHOMA VALLEY

I see the farms have closed-up shop,
The houses button-up like strangers,
The hog's deflowered by December,
And time descends in icy drops.

Yet, seasonless, the boys never rest,
But as I did, over snow,
By windmills and bare scrub oak,
Run like songs in maidens' breasts.

ON A RANCH EAST OF TOWN

Though empty clouds boomed warnings
Of the sun's aztecal pyramids,
Big-handed men shouldered here
With their horse-drawn ships;
Though the winds were freebooters
And coyotes cried warnings,
Horse and D-8 driven like galleys
Left wakes of long furrows
From prows of their gangplows;
Many dreams died,
Saluted by volleys of dust;
And droughts longer than anchors
Decayed whole cargoes of men;
Vortices blackly lashed their houses,
Wrecking them like lifeboats
On shoals of cottonwoods.

IF HARVEST IS LATE

Cherish the dried husk,
There's some yellow corn inside;
There still might be some reaping.
While stalk stands, I mutter,
Some corn outlasts the drought;
You work real hard with these husks,
Though they're streaked with rain,
You'll get a pile of yellow grains.

To hell with hope,
There is nothing so miserable
Or phoney as that waiting sneak,
If harvest is so lousy late,
I'll plow you under;
A soul plants many egos,
Expects a few to fail.

SPRING

You shameless goat!
Even as young calves bawl
Bulls paw new pasture;
In phalanx-speared grass
Subtle seeds corkscrew dig;
Muddy sluck or sandy swash,
Green and many pipes your spawn.

You swagger!
Flinging freely
Songs of meadowlarks,
Showering softly
Rains of violets,
Weaving weeds and creeds
In fabrics from the dust.

You uncorked bubble!
Sweeter than Chablis
Your truths of sky,
Redder than Port
Your bravados of wind;
Did you need winter's cellar
To ferment so rich a drunk?

QUATRAIN

Dry books and school
Ever make a fool
Of laughing song.
So, they are wrong!

TO LUCKY YOUNG MEN AND WOMEN

Because the heart has been trained
    you may unleash it!
Because the mind has been disciplined
    you may dream;
Because the body was hardened
    you may enjoy;
Because the soul was formed then,
    and the soul guides now.

LEBENSRAUM

As a child,
On a board with clay
I marshalled Alexandrian empires;

In my teens,
Roaming the western states
I was passion's Khan;

Now,
suave with galaxies,
From this cell I plot escape.

II

HYBRIS

Blood,
Salty child of ocean,
Surges the immense advance,
While grassy rock
Revolves our ceremony
Through fire-warped space
Which, eye-stabbed, collapses,
Conquered, on our flesh --
That fawning liar till its death.

Illusion urged are we
By this benign trinity
Of sky and rock and sea.

Who dares blame our arrogance?
Deep time-rooted,
Rhythmic with elemental motion,
Darlings of evolution --
Why deny desire?
Veins and eye
Say yes to reddest thoughts.
Are they death's dupes?
Cannot the moment pinnacle
Despite all reason, somehow,
To a truth?

SIRIUS IS A DOUBLE STAR

Sirius imbrued burnt-out buildings
With myth's white blood,
For arm in arm we strode
Down Michigan Avenue
Picked up from three a.m. corners,
Rescued from the early news.

We surveyed our sudden rendezvous,
Surrendered lakeward stars
Pause due the map of time,
Then turned to the silent Avenue
By which hustling people had paid,
Chattering, their hours out
To buy a city day,
Humble to honking horns,
But we, like country pagans,
Exultant at ageless rites,
Deemed incense all reek
Of sacrifice smearing this
Milkless, uplifted Loop.

WASHINGTON SQUARE, CHICAGO, U.S.A.
(drawn from scenes of 1951)

I heard an old man crack jokes
(An old musket clicking --
Pioneer powder gone dead)
On a box at bughouse square --
The dean of all those who spoke
    at Free Speech Square --
On my left an old worker
Eyes still smoldering with ancient glow
(Remembering Big Bill roar
    on yellow-ugly Butte plateau --)
On my right a young girl in daring cape,
Laughing to her adoring escort,
It's really true,
They do talk radical about our money
    here on Washington Square --
A busload of tourists pulls up
And, prepping for Europe, they gawk to satisfy
Elkian, Moosian, Zoolike curiosity that:
The government really does let those damn Reds
    rave right here on a Chicago square.
(The old dean got around to anarchy and peace)
A young man follows with tears,
O Christian daring to be a Christian O!
That a mob burnt a black man's residence,
That the world, or many of its cylinders at least,
    is run by the hissing heat of hate.
He loves the freedom here and speaking
To two hundred of Chicago's millions
    rejoices in the glory of Bughouse Square.

O patch of sidewalk, grass, and homos!
Showplace of the First Amendment
And Jefferson's rusty monument!
O place of voices,

Voices of the past, the dead, the dying,
And here and there, it may be,
Somewhat of tomorrow and today,
Voices behind bars of separation,
From the tourists, slummers, bums,
Old workers, and teething intellects,
From the one hundred!
Plot of legalized rant,
Mad hymn to the reddened sky,
Defying forty miles of steel
With voices, a box, a corner lamp --

O Free Speech Square!

CLARK STREET, CHICAGO

The Street skids on its wrinkled face,
No mudpacks would do it any good,
There's no beauty to restore,
Not in its hawking throat,
Nor in its limp skin of stagger,
Nor in that revolving eye of Law
Inflamed above the Paddy Wagon --
By moustached Stripteasers
I've reached all that I can take,
"Get it over with, Clark Street, die!"

But voices, blooms from weedy men,
With a dime's confidence ask, "Coffee";
On cracked lips of building rows
Dawn lights peaceful cigarettes --
The Street's crumpled face
Is but the face I've often glimpsed
Behind a gaily mirrored mask.

And dying compels tenderness --
Thoughtfully, Clark Street,
I pace by your lame lurch,
Sit by dirty cots of cafes
Awkward as an untrained nurse,
And pity also cops and preachers
Who with fists and ignorant fingers
Gouge your sores.

ESCAPE IN MARGINS

Those who duel life
Without seconds or mediation,
Who accompany clouds
On shiftless voyages
From unpoliced ports,
Are vagabonds
Who might be epic,
But socially are taboo,
At best to docile children
A television fairy tale.

Men who survive in rocks
Are not, of course, protected
Any more than prairie wolves
For they, too, can be marauders.
A little free because mostly lost,
Because, roaming oreless canyons,
They don't get in the customary clubs,
They find escape in margins
And shelter between the lines.

But in deserts where empires
Shrink to sherds, genteel notions vanish;
They way you lug your gear looms large.

HUMAN DIALECTIC

I can love lies,
Get drunk on easy dreams,
Embrace misery,
That undemanding slut,
And find catastrophe itself,
Self-killer of self-despair,
Hardly awes my face
Thickened with tallow years
Till proof against hottest tears.

I also run in wolfpacks
That survive this bloodless meat --
Outside fearful circles
Of our fires, amid snarls,
Frozen urine, stale wild odor,
And lip-drawn twitch at pitchy smoke,
I find back beyond the tribe,
Before the first great masks were carved:
Hackles stiff with surge,
And stars seen for what they urge.

Between decorous wax
Languid with neon thrills
And the lean wolves
Foraging my gut,
I admit a tenacious seed,
A speck of Self;
If it should ever bloom,
A burning bush from my desert sides,
I fall down amazed,
Bruise my knees, and prophesy for days.

EMILY DICKINSON

She lives in light!
A faceted sight,
An ice-lit ocean,
Emerald's devotion --

The sun's health --
Vulgar wealth
By aim so clear,
Resolve so rare.

THE HUNTER

Do not watch the stars.
They, too, pass away,
But during your life
Orion will dazzle changeless,
Made formal by the Greeks,
Mythical by time;
And your intensest past,
The far-different past
When these suns
Were merely light
In a certain bright array
Will, on Antaean haunches,
Howl, wolflike,
From forgotten patterns
Of blood and thought.

Do not watch the stars.
During your life
Orion will always
Center the January night,
Will reshape old questions
Into old mauls.

III

NIGHT SONG

Crumple me up the cubic worlds,
The lonely law-padded cages;
Let hot black mate cold black,
And do it on volcanic stages.

Crumple me up the cubic worlds,
All prophets with iron moulds,
The tinsel, gouty cannon,
And men who can be bought and sold.

TO PALLAS ATHENE

I have sailed such oceans
As would have made Magellan pause
Though I may die myself
On some uncharted Philippines
And beneath stars unknown to Palomar.

Yet, befriended by bearded sea dogs,
Lost in revels bought by rubies,
I can hear the song, though faintly,
That made Odysseus bind himself
Against the siren voices,
And leave his nymph, Calypso.

CONVERSATION IN CAMBRIDGE

She talked with a stutter to people,
She talked without a stutter to her bird,
He was from Haiti, a cockatoo,
He never stuttered as he sang.

The old woman in tweeds
And he in his green feathers,
Separated by a window from Boston snow,
She talked and he sang, back and forth,
She alone from other people,
He from other cockatoos,
She talked and he sang, back and forth.

MORNING THOUGHTS
IN A STEEL MILL

Imagination is not all,
Nor health, nor mind,
Nor bold bravery,
No, nor all these together
Alloy the strength
We call a man;

The finest heat of steel,
From point of potential,
Can be scrapped
From half-percent of dirt,
Twenty minutes sleep
That ruin a shift;

It takes control
To steady final pour,
Deslag youth's furnace,
Blow the stringers,
Take out the brittle
To roll our shape.

SONG HEARD IN PITTSBURGH

Somewhere in these skyscrapers is Truth!
But our aluminum shouts
Mirror the stainless facts,
And sterile as glass window
We never see blood on concrete.

We have found that bridges
Don't span the difficult rivers,
That days die in traffic jams;
We race on drunken nights
Around circles of cloverleafs.

The clothes we wear away are flesh;
And though we don French styles
To mask our shriveling hide,
More Spartan that we think,
We go to graves on shields of metal dreams.

TO METAL

Toughy substance
Rock-hidden
Fire-born
Hammer-shaped
Die-drawn;
Blaze, crackle, pour --
Lean, smooth, and honed.
Metal!
Silent race of slaves;
Not volunteers,
Hard conquests
Ripped from mountain forts,
Fracturing in mute rebellion,
Combining with gases
In surreptitious flight.
Metal!
Oscillating nuclei
Phalanx strong
Ignoring the electron swarm,
Platonic cubes
From random statistics,
Triumph of equations,
Miracle of enigmas;
With X-Ray and sledgehammer
We caress these lovely hunks of
Metal!
Barbaric bronze,
Democratizing iron,
Revolutionary steel,
River-bottom plower,
Planetary prow --
Imperial veteran,
Stained with sweat and silicosis,
To challenge space itself.

OFTEN I COUNT UP MY MISTAKES,

Take stock of my depleted name,
Figure the years to pay my debts,
Add and subtract like a dumb machine
Known fragments of an unknown whole,
Forever see the figures red,
Deficit and bankruptcy by any system,
Yet but to write your name
Lends such prestige to my insolvency,
That I clap shut the books and shout, I'm sound!

THERE HAVE BEEN

A billion billion loves
Since that hominoid throb
First mixed sex and thought,
And a thousand languages,
And a million poems,
Yet I tell you
I've never heard or read
Or seen our double;
Though in statistic's name,
How can we, our value, be unique?
I don't know.
But we are.

ARS LONGA

There is something in art
Stiffer, colder than the heart;
Its honed rhythm of neglect
Prunes feelings to select,
For though highest emotions tire,
Measure and melody mustn't mar.

A lover fleeing jealous love,
I stalk the streets in wild divorce,
And mock in bars what makes me move.

Inhuman as all transcendence must be,
Art demands strict monogamy;
A marriage with no rights of bed,
A marriage careless of daily bread,
A marriage with frigid lover,
A marriage over which disasters hover,
A marriage with such rare delights
It's worth the chill of most the nights.

MOON IN MANHATTAN

From sheared, angled, mangled sky
Fall scraps and remnants
Almost bright as airplanes
Or windowlights,
And these shreds
Whet the whirling cutters
Especially after bars close down.
Nonetheless, when a brassy cocktail
Perches round and red
Upon the clamorous rim of Houston Street
It pours the same intoxication
That twice rooted me
Through all a mountain night.

KIWI

In sawdust days
We suckled the beer we drank
And traced pools of spill
Into dark abstracts
Astonishing the wooden bar
The traffic light flashed
Green yellow red green yellow red
An action painter off his head
And over dirty slush
Yellow headlights glared rush
And hard toward destinies
We never cared to guess
Admiring through the fishnet frosted window
Their stop start speed slow
The universe put on its show.

SEAN O'CASEY -- MEMORIAM

You loudmouth laugher
    at sell-out and dreamer;
you brazen clatter
    through
    pubhouse, flats, and fighting talk;
you hopeless reveler of hopes, faithful
    witness of the faithless, loving lasher
    of unloving and unlashed;
you heller at the wake, explosion
    in the cathedral, riot in the repression;
you damned old codger, insolent poet, fire;
you ignite me.

TO ERNEST HEMINGWAY

You would not hurry;
Life is short, but you took the time
To rewrite and rewrite and rewrite
Until words attained the same importance
As death and wine and love.

A MOTHER

Old Lady, how young you are!
I caught that girlish glint,
Wrinkles, frailty, grey don't hide it,
Not even worries over saccharine and diet;
You mischievously observe your son,
Though it's now forty years in all
Since the first rambunctious squall.
Why, old mother, must we wither,
Why is it not enough to die?

AN ENDING

There are days, my friend,
In which Time, aghast,
Reels backwards to a start --
That germ, then, is finished, done!

Incredulous, something dies
That thought itself as young as us,
And before its eyes, also ours,
Its completed life is seen.

And many a midnight's spent
To record such histories,
For not often does Time
Pause long enough for men to think.

WALL STREET, NEW YORK

What holds together all the skyscrapers
Of the individual speculation?
Who'll pay to dig the public subways
To communicate from mind to mind?
Anyhow, they'd connect us
With our neighbors' slums --
Build a suburban bridge with sex?
Profits are mink to wife -- or mistress.
Brag in unheard alternation at our bars,
Energy, energy, is what we've got to sell;
Why, dam it steep up here,
Charge higher the electric thrill,
And cheer the foaming crash.

METAPHOR IN SKID ROW

Entombed within the shrouding skull
On which soft flesh grew,
Subtle ideas decayed, became dull.
Seasons of drunkenness and new
Loves (though only a wharf front trull)
Came and left the flesh a faintly mounting clue
Of that absolute death
When within deep planetary rock
Bones lie free from fevered breath,
And vaster seasons mock
The small variety which flesh beneath
Had strived to gain -- within a city block.
And subterranean echoes of this mighty change
Gave this derelict such range
That, drunken in a park, a falling leaf
Seemed terrible, cold, and strange.

THE EXECUTIVE

He dealt with many faces;
So he preferred his women in the dark
And his lonely office above a park.

He dealt with many faces;
They stiffened formal as cards,
Marked kings and deuces, trumps or discards.

He dealt with many faces;
They divided into dull or conniving blank,
And his grew bland and cruel with rank.

HERO

Dare dreams,
dream destiny,
destine mind,
mind body,
body a crown,
crown blooms,
bloom phallus,
impregnate centuries.

BEING-UNTO-DEATH HEIDDEGER

Will I kiss her
Knowing I must die
Then it is good.

Will I speak now
Knowing I must die
Then it is good.

Will I sit here
Knowing I must die
Then it is good.

Will I strike him
Knowing I must die
Then it is good.

Will I live on
Knowing I must die
Then it is good.

IV

LEAVING TANGIER

No one to know how far ventured conquest
Past last sighting
Latitude/Longitude respect to another losing sailor
But *I know* undiscovered continents abound
I will escape feudal panoplies of myth
Light purple dawns over Rabat
Cafe au lait long dead (O night-time cities
Chicagos of waiting fit only for writing)
In whom feel my hard embrace
Take back response
Reconfirmation born again
Die again Dying's life
In death no dying
Rabat Marrakech Chicago Uravan Paul's Valley, Oklahoma
All tufts trickles slurp slop
You each trivial magnificence
Even you scrofula impetigo and all things
From the old four dimensional weary Egyptian world
You'll wear me out at last
But no other racecourse recourse do have
So I pay for coffee, count my change
and venture out.

CHICAGO REMEMBERED IN BANGKOK

That ancient luring light
of rain and tram and car
don't care of rushing-by;
squeegie rubbing out the clatter
of lonely slammed-down coffee
on greasy tabletops
where hope climbs past garbage
on back apartment steps
to radio, beer, and plastic couch
where gaunt penned dreams
rub razorbacks snortling round
the creaking bed
while through torn curtains
the steel on steel
racket spluttered rain
creeps in, grey grey grey and wet.

EAGLE

The full moon backed down like an
    old catfish into a flood-caved bank;
Morning's minnows broke surface;
Grasshoppers with winking lights
    we whirred toward the padi;
Two oxcarts beetled down the
    tiny path worn in wet lawns;
Machine gunners poked around the
    brushpiles of treelines;
First for the boy;
He wondered and prepared about death;
Alive, chopping back to base,
He burst into sun
And lit a cigarette on landing.

DEATH OF A MONTAGNARD KO HO

The boy trembled as if shaken by an angry father,
his throat filled up choked by manufactures
    of his own body,
the flesh wore off his buttocks and back,
    sheets abrasive as sandpaper
        after a week,
his mother, father, and grandmother slept on mats
    at the foot of his cot,
it was hopeless from the beginning,
the clinic was shorthanded,
flung down there in the mountains,
a nurse invented a device to clear his throat,
the doctor, two nurses, and technician went
    on round the clock,
their regular duties continued,
day after day the body shook, the throat filled,
the IV dropped into him, the watchers suctioned
    out the passageway,
after thirteen days and nights it ended,
he died easily in his sleep,
the mother and father had reconciled themselves,
by that time the professionals took it hard.

TO_____

The old woman wasn't bent double --
near as I could tell she was only bent
    85 degrees from the vertical --
a kind of roughened back, almost scaly,
blind I suppose from childhood,
the doctor used terms like pellagra and trachoma,
actually I don't think he listened to his words
    any more than I did,
the old woman had made it up from the river behind the village
they said by herself
but they had to steer her to the spot on the bench
to face the stethoscope and probe
there in that hut with the foxhole shelter dug just outside
only the doctor just rose and said
it isn't necessary
tell the mothers and young girls to look at old woman here
when their eyes turn red
use aureomycin
his voice had the control needed to keep down screams
to hold back tears
to avoid all sentimentality
help her back he said
to the river where the white geese float beneath the
    paired log foot bridge
later that day at night Christmas Eve we called it
we talked, ate well, remembered what we knew of nostalgia,
rambling back to those non-trachomaed days
in American fields colleges and homes
but where even we nonetheless were crippled.

45

BRIGHT-VEDA

Sun is bright
bright the stars
bright and hot is fire
bright is eye
and bright the diamond
dew is bright
and lightning
and waterfall are bright
and lamps and neon
and polished steel are bright
and bright the axe sound
over frozen snow.

OBIT

On that muddy Hoogly surf
the Calcutta sky took off
with flaming flesh
that'd dropped its soul
and stoned the trams in broken fury
and knelt to worn-out gods
and slucked up a million teas
in tiny crowded shops
and drove the rusting cabs in honking splendor
past the rickshaw runners sinking in the mud.

ONE MINUTE AT AGRA

Red assed monkeys scratched their
    sprawled-out legs;
The jammed bitch trudged pulling
    her ribby male;
The bicycle rickshaw driver coughed
    in the acrid and animal traffic;
The Taj limned blue geometries hard against the hazy highs
    while the dark horizon growled;
Three-year-olds screeched jungle
    clutching marble lattice;
The Jumuna swirled filthy glitter,
    scraps on the holy flood.

ONE SONG OF INDIA

The frogs croaked lakes of sound,
the banyan tree lived on its roots
      after dying at the core,
temples buried the Buddha,
the monsoons shifted to the east,
Shiva became restricted to six arms,
      ten forms, and twenty-four incarnations,
those who stood on the diamond point
      of the universe fell to the Chinese,
at night where creeks began among the rocks
      drums still beat and bells rang,
in purple Calcutta dusk rotting to black
      white figures hurried to doom, joy, or
routine,
one man moved like a leech,
      lying down, drawing feet to his head,
      standing up, aimed for richer-than-blood,
palpable clouds pushed north
      for days, a season, recurrent years,
      ages, always a catchless moment,
those who found something
      stared out of self-engravings
      and bestowed their finished beauty,
others sought out incense,
      gold, silver, deep long-throated horns,
and crimson chalk
      to stroke their bouqueted gods.

49

STATUE OF BUDDHA, BOMBAY

Torn from context of contemplation,
fragment pushed into pellmell ...
Lord Buddha with one hand broken,
not the late fat
    but the young strong Buddha --
It was welcome news
thought possessed such thews.

V

LIPS

Thrifty Swiss lips, calculating precise profit on passion
French lips, a la mode, with rhetoric of glory
English lips, savoring gazumping their contract
German lips, drunken, natural, and treacherous
American lips, advertising bargains galore buyers beware
Hindu lips, offering cosmic illusion, bliss, bliss, bliss
Chinese lips, practical, delivering the necessary
Slavic lips, gulps of vodka, moon on the Volga
Black lips, signalling "I'm on to your scam but here I am!"
Arab lips, beheaded and beheading, minarets lost in Allah

INTERZONE

Days of Poesy
were contrabanded
into blue plutonium nights
where european civilisation
bombed out in ecstasy
and naked tradition
danced again with the up to date
and to create
did not call in judge jury and killer dogs
and the morning contemplated
results called crime
in all the capitals of destruction
and found them laughing
and beautiful as boys -- dance on beachsand
the berbers sold figs dates
goatcheese roundbaked bread tangerines
and threw in a way of being for free
no transformation shocked your friends
who also disappeared into the new
even the secret police
became part of the scene
and had their assigned seats
on socco chico
where the action went a little public
hinting of the magic rooms
where laws of identity,
repealed,
no longer caricatured the living faces,
where time, wealth, power and rage
merged again with flesh
connected with the polymetric rhythms
"how can I get it for you
if you don't tell me what you want?"
in Interzone he who could word
the yet undreamt
kinged it
providing the dreams for the day.

SUBWAY!

Subway!
Ever' body don't have a car
Or a taxi
Or a limousine
Or a pad close to work
Too much hurry for a bus
Like all of us
Gets on the subway!
We're all down here together,
We've escaped the weather!
Swaying' and touchin'
Bumpin' and lookin'
Readin' and meditatin'
Dreamin' and steamin'
Groanin' and moanin'
Waitin' for downtown
Or the Village
Waitin' for the City
Don't give us no pity
We're here 'cause
This is where it's at:
Manhattan!
New York, New York,
Fame around the corner
Billions in the sky
Sex in every eye
Where you can stake out
You can make out
You can shake out
Let it all hang out
Do your thing
Be discovered
Get mugged
Or drugged
Meet the public

Damn the republic
Be nice
Or live with lice
Down here in the subway
You're so low
Everybody's in the underground
But nobody gives a graffiti
We're free
To survive if we can
Create if we must
Dawn to dawn and dust to dust.

MR. KABUKI

Mr Kabuki
Saw the vacant mind of that Western chick
Said Baby I'm moving in I know what makes you tick.
But Mr. Kabuki
Didn't know her body filled with fidgets
Her tongue busy busy busy with complaints
Mr. Kabuki
Now would rather manufacture widgets
Than deal with would-be saints
Hard to take science to the East?
Try enlightenment to the West.
Mr. Kabuki
Has only theater left
In Tokyo he gasps for breath
In New York he sees the living death
But on the stage he'll take those chicks
And shape them up or ship them to the flicks
Never look into another empty brain
Til muscles move to mathematics
And tongues speak subtly sane,
Mr. Kabuki smiles his smile
And whiles away his while.

RIFF OF BOBBY BUNSEN

I'm becoming deaf dumb and blind
getting older
Must become bolder.
A rat
With my yellow alley cat.
Collective solipsism's not my mind.
Pestilential world
That evolved the glorious plague of humanity.
Aphorisms of the unpublished preposterous.

****

Revenge! Revenge! Revenge!
Humanity at present weighs four hundred billion pounds,
Increasing eighty billion pounds per year.
Hardly time to shove in a painless death.
Why are you so jittery?
The tension glamorous and profitable.
Make babies. Make babies.
Man horrified, helpless from conception to death.
I could scream but I'm gonna smile,
Can't tell the shit from the shinola
Bangin' to the last on the pianola!

****

I can dance!
I'm on to your scam but here I am!
Why should I front for you?
I need help on a special project.
This special project reports to SURVIVAL.
In the competitive matrix of a planet of catastrophe.
Nothing would appear bizarre
At a point of total collapse.
The show's not allowed to stop
One OD's another takes her place
And whenever there's a flop
They hustle in new Pretty Face.

Mister, based on repression and triviality,
I bought the ground out from under you.
You gotta go sooner or later.
The breakdown of the Compromise.
Won't come back without friends.
I probably can but what if I can't?
Encore! Encore! Encore!
The real scoop. You know what I mean.
I pinpointed the origin of paranoia
And it led straight to you.
Shut up and dance
Movement's the real trance.

****

I'm gonna throw away the keys,
Bulldoze this place down,
And then you'll be on the street,
And it's illegal to be on the street.
I'll wipe you out with the latest from Destruction Dynamics.
Rev it up, Harry!
Only in the tools of the Night
Will you find the empire to fight.
Defenses flash; they want some too
They can't get it because they don't know
Gasoline cuisine go go go.

****

Male bond and the thrill of team play
Real power of dualities
Dream of paradoxes that wreck your intelligentsia with Truths
Little ol' Texas is actually a spaceship in disguise
Preliminary shock wave calculated to rupture your confidence
We will now have to be given the full countdown
All that's really needed is Us
I propose to end my Heart's Desire
And to reconstitute the whole sorry show.

Two universes can't be in Time at once
All it costs are my convictions.
(A slug of my latest researches
Known to go with perfect health.)
As long as you work with half-baked types
You have to expect certain forms to reach for power, too.
Do I look like a fall guy?
I thought it all meant something
Well, that was a real comedy.
The Price of Progress would like to speak to you.

****

I've paid the price. I feel it in my bones.
A sunk cost,
Of no calculable importance to dynamic leaders.
Shoulda gone to the Institute of Technology.
Harvard, the rootless masses of Higher Criticism
Our work has only just begun.
Hopefully more advanced than baboons.
At last! My frontier!
Commence the Countdown, Mac!
Behind the safety shield!
I'll do the final check.
We left the planet at daylight
Headed for the stars.

VI

AFTER A LIFE OF ACTION

After a life of action what have I learned?
I have learned to walk to sit to stand to lie down
And that silence ranks above talk
But that poetry's best
And like all best is rare
And to be treasured savored and used
For it is the fish that can feed the five thousand
And will never wear out
But grow more interesting with time
Alone of all man's works escaping entropy
An end in itself
A joy to enjoy
Poetry can be lost but never destroyed
In the ecology of man poetry is the indicator species
Of the health of the dream.

THE FIRESIDE, 1985

By essence!
Who would've thought we'd make it,
The ship's crew arrested at Aruba and headline framed,
The ship sunk at mid-tide level off the Kimberly Coast
Among the mud and mangroves,
Reefed again and broken-hulled on a mud flat at Bawean,
The Captain hauled off at Crete on trumped-up charges
To do a term with sodomizers of goats and killers of girls,
Steel-scow smashed and holed in the Amazon
With its great oily whirlpools interrupting the red-brown roar,
Crashed into Savaii's basaltic reef,
Brought off amid the breakers, a two month battle,
The rabble at Galle on their Tamil-plundering spree
Racing for the dock, the ship casting off just ahead of
                              shouted screams,
The sliding anchor on the Force 10 squall
Hurling it toward greasy rocks in Bombay's slimy waters,
The days when money had gone and no more came
When beans, tea, and cheap bananas remained the only grub
                              in a gonorrheaic port.
Well, on it sailed, and traversed the planet,
Monsoons, Westerlies, the Trades, the Doldrums, Currents,
                              Rivers and Reefs,
Borne onward ten years and a hundred thousand miles,
First upon the dreams of Conrad, Rimbaud, Cook and Darwin,
Then having eaten those dreams dreams its own way onward,
On glorious tides raised and lowered by sublunar Nostalgia.

NIGHT

Dreams daubed resplendent prospects of unhampered wealth,
While Sleep pulled out the connections to the symbolic computer,
Then Archetypes on the loose trampled down pity and terror,
Those pseudo-saints of the incipient soul;
I faced sex and death without orgasm or convulsion,
Thought scudded, unmoored from logic,
Desire cycloned, unballasted of education,
Emotion rocketed past gravity to that place where all
directions are equal,
Sweetness beyond sugar drenched my blood.
I still possesed a future!
The New would again wreak
Its havoc unequally, upon me and my world
Changing both into that state beyond ecstatic grace,
Where freedom lays destiny on the line
Handing out the choice choice
And the time for decision falls like the guillotine.

REVERIES OF THE TRANSLUNAR INTELLECT

"The conquered forgot their conquerors
But the conquerors never forgot their conquered."

MESSAGE FOUND ENGRAVED IN PLATINIM
ON EXTRATERRESTIAL SPACESHIP X09

Truth was it that we sought and fought for?
Power and even powers arrived
And the world glittered in freshness
That beseeched the name Eternal.
Insights forwarded our actions.
And action produced new insights.
In the lover's bed of Succeed
Undreamed dreams conceived
Undone doings
And except for the vast disorder that Time
Discards throughout Space
Nothing could disturb the splendor.
Time that threatens
The transcendental substance
That the Unfathomable uses to achieve its Glory
Can hardly fail to annihilate our moments,
Make cacophony of sweetest modes,
Render Beauty and Metaphysics
As powerless of certainty as a kiss;
Dramatic danger
Sums our understanding's Truth,
And leaves our synergy its only hope;
Every part and all the parts await their doom,
Only the unpredictable ignites Freedom.

THE DOOR

The intensity required
To walk through an open door
That leads to the new
Must shatter the gentle habit
And the angry explosion alike
Since alertness and spontaneity
Alone answer the demand
Never before heard,
The deal never before offered,
Admit an as-yet uncalculated force
To spin the I into a gyre
To take up unfamiliar quarters,
Command an unknown ship
Through unmapped seas
Toward ports of grim and alluring legend.

RECORD

How one searched,
Going far beyond those who accepted
The small carrots and big sticks
Of the conquerors
Whose lifetimes passed
In negotiating increases of ten-per-cent in carrot size;
Searching, one saw the four realms,
Touched earth, tasted water, smelled air, and heard the fire,
But finally realized the fear of finding
Kept us moving down the streets, as beggarly
         as when we had begun.
Oh, we found things, burnished, broken,
Inscrutable, geometrical things, some of them
Enduring four billion years with passive affirmation;
We found energies, and sent messages to the stars;
History, and rewrote not only fate but even
Revised a line or two of destiny;
Values, and with this great secret
Motivated hierarchal wars beyond Genghiz Khan's ambitions;
Intelligence that could accomplish fantasy's obscurest impulses;
The Irrational that found paradox a commonplace,
And only the discontinuous truly interesting;
And Life that ate the sun, the earth, the moon,
Crawled from the water, ran on the land, flew in the air,
And extracted in space;
We became richer than misers and kingdoms and alchemists
Yes, golden girls and boys,
Living in golden dawns
Loving in golden sunsets
We purchased without care or calculations, freely,
Daily minted new delights
From the enigmatic Treasury of our golden world.
But we understood nothing,
And the spider enwebbed our treasure

64

Strewn about in total entropy of all its information.
Once we had understood we did not understand
We gave up our hoards to living masters
Who flung updated ancient texts at us to study
Throughout the nights and years and crowds of unseen
                    contemporary phenomena,
Until India became a family slaughter at Kurukshetra
China a cypress tree blowing in a courtyard,
Khorassan a blue and golden lion eating hearts,
Egypt a shadow aligned with a crack in the world's pavement,
And America a rite of passage.
Then, happy as children,
We pointed at this and that and not-this and not-that
Wordless, timeless, placeless,
Ensconced upon a throne that could not be overthrown.
Some stayed on in that wonderful City
But the rest of us sensed
That the source of these delightful fountains
And those who architected their ever-changing forms
Could not be reached within any walls so-ever.
We advanced toward ecstasy
With minds that now could not be blown;
Only by standing outside ourselves, those hazy atmospheres,
Could genuine astronomy be studied
And the real world charted for further expeditions.
Not to seek, not to find, not to understand,
Not-this, not-this, not-this, a severe awakeness,
Till our physiology reached total go, and we total stop,
Only at this point could we perceive;
Separated from hopeful fear and fearful hope,
From misery and from bliss,
From existence, we saw ... ourselves and all
The turning world that turned us and epi-turns
That we turned the world, and the epi- epi-turns ...
And then we saw ... nothing.
Some quickly turned down their glance
And became death-in-life and life-in-death,

Still as death in their trance and quick as life with their gay malice;
Their needs found disciples who purchased a sense of proportion.
We did not experience life, nor existence,
But yellow without substance heat or light,
Discipline without effort, reward, or disappointment,
Sublimity without art, science, or adventure,
Friendship without doing anything for anyone or accepting
anything from anyone,
Beauty without form or relationship, omnipresent and powerless,
Luck that brought us no applause, advantage, or position.
Then some of us began to serve nothing and no one.
We brought all our searches
And they lit up a red that told us everything,
We brought all our findings
And they revealed a white that reconciled us to everything,
We brought all our understanding
And they attracted a black that gave us peace,
We brought our nothing to Nothing
And Nothing did not increase nor did it change,
But green spread its bannerless banner
Between yellow and red and white and black.
We had found the origin of Everything,
And the end of Everything,
And Everything, All Existence, became the apparatus of our being,
And then though we used all that we could use
Of knowledge, ecstasy, and work,
Secretly we depended upon nothing,
And we had escaped and were free,
And all we wished to do was to satisfy nothing
As nothing had satisfied us
And we were emperors-of-the-world
Beneath a blackberry bush
And passed inordinate decrees
About how our music must be thus-and-so
To make the Nightclub of the Caravan of Dreams,
And, laughing, you might find us anywhere.

THE AMERICANS
Dedicated to the Policies of Openness in Russia and China

The Americans watch while they work,
The Americans vote on the devotees of power,
Between tweedledee and tweedledum
    Many vote 50-50 by not voting,
Americans vote by voting and buying in America
    And by buying and selling in the world
    And by not buying and not-selling,
The Americans opulently slouch
    Or rigorously lengthen their spine
They pay for their mistakes
    By going bankrupt or hitting the road.
The Americans revere the five or six presidents
    Who helped them forge their reality,
The rest they consign to oblivion
    After a momentary fame,
    The cruelest punishment they can imagine
The Americans welcome every sign
    Of openness and generosity in their opponents
And quickly say get lost
    To a friend who becomes pushy.
The Americans standing on a street corner,
    Sprawled in front of their TV, laid
    Back in their touch controlled car, striding
    Around their workspace with voice and fingers
    Networked to the globe, watch
    Out of the corner of their eyes,
They don't suffer fools gladly and hate
    Phonies with the passion of artists,
    And oppressors with the wrath of god,
They admire those who fight back,
    And help those who hurt.

The Americans try out every image
    They can dream of in the

Phantasmagoria of the
Inexhaustibility of phenomena
Fleeting across their looking-glasses,
And don't take it so serious,
The Americans stash away every
Gambler's trick, sex gambit, dollar
Play, power game, montage, shrewd
Remark, and abandoned moment
They can lay their hands on, erecting
Personal skyscrapers of potentiality that the
Manhattan skyline only faintly mirages,
The Americans act free not because of any
Of the above, but because they know
That on the wild side, they can be down
But never out, they can pick themselves
Up and start all over again in the
Magnificently evolving universe their
Society's chaotic cosmos imitates, that
New roles always wing their way
Toward them from the theater of all
Luck, chances, and opportunities,
The Americans do the impossible because
They live in the future where the
Rules can be changed and do change,
They laugh going broke or all the way to the bank,
And wryly joke to the moment of battle itself.

The Americans, comrades, know that they are the
Revolution and they welcome you
Joining in on the fun and excitement
You are destroying those rulers that
Bowed your necks to their decreed limits,
Just as we did in 1776, 1861, 1933, and 1967.
The Americans offer you and anyone else
An open hand to the open road
Winding through the spectaculars
Of dangerous, yielding, and surprising

Time-Space-Energy-Life.
The Americans no more than you
      Know what we will do or find along the way
      But the Americans smile and say, OK, let's go.

DREAMS

If life is a dream
Why dream so few dreams?
All out for dreams!
Dreams go all out!
Dreams exist, dreams follow laws,
Dreamtime, dreamspace,
What dreams can dreams dream?
Put dreams into action
Then actions live and dreams go on the learning curve.
I dream therefore I become.
Dream! Let dreams act on your will.
I have nothing to lose but an old dream.
Don't go to sleep when I dream,
Dreams too interesting to be left to the sleeping,
Dreamer, awake! ... to my dreams.
I dream that I am a dreamer.
Whose dreams make a synergy with all dreamers.
Architecture and love ... too precious to be spent on less
than a dream.
Dreams make brighter colors.
Dreams show forms that hurl one from the sickbed.
Dreams take emotions past illusion to realized power.
Dreams develop the intellect with the defiance of their designs.
Dreams reveal destiny, lightnings beyond consciousness.
I can only live in a dream, New York is only a budget.
Appear to me in a dream and I adore you.
Appear to me as a dreamer, I will follow you anywhere.
Dreams, beyond magic, religion, and science,
Dreams, revelations so gorgeous we forget what they revealed,
Therefore dreams, I always wait, on fire for new dreams.

IN THE SONORAN DESERT

In the Sonoran desert
The rock ridges fall to the salt beaches
Hawks watch for a rabbit amongst the ocotillo
Rattlesnakes coil in the shade of mesquite
White owls swoop silently on moonlit mice
Opuntia feeds the javelina
Tony Burgess looks for a new species
And I search for a poem
The little flowers open after a little rain
The wind raises dust down the coyote tracked arroyo
Noon forces a hot quietness into every patch of green
Blazes from micaceous sand
Skunks and scorpions stroll proud tails upraised
A cloud of midges circles my sweat
An Indian finds his peyote prepares to eat the flesh of god
In the Sonoran desert
I lay down with a bottle of red wine
On the moonwhite sand in a small arroyo
At the age of seventeen and an hour later
Gazing upward saw the stars white stars many white stars
So many white flashing tender stars
I never moved till red chill light
Snatched them away and I got up remembering perfection.

THE HIGHER PROPAGANDAS

Of course rage and hate held revolution
The only manly answer to rampant injustice;
Better to die a snarling wolf
Than whimpering lapdog deformed by crazy genetics;
Sorrow cried that help alone
Held the keys and title to nobility
And obliged and guided by fellow-felt compassion
Should join the brotherhood of poverty and agony,
Ceaselessly sharing throughout the killings, cripplings,
        and not-enough;
Love praised self-absorption into the Object,
The subject disappeared, subjection stopped,
I transform into Not-I, Not-I becomes then also I,
And I escaped by sublime dialectic to I am that I am,
        Sacrifice yourself for the glory of yourself,
"If I make my love glow, then I am that lovely glow";
Beauty built a pyramid in Egypt,
A wall in China, a statue in Mexico;
Each glimpse of his nakedness through the fabulous garment, a
Seamless alignment of intentions, attention, and extension
Created a senseless silence,
A stop to the cycles of sacrifice, compassion, revolution;
A glance of a beautiful woman,
Allowing no hope of embrace from love, compassion or rape,
Robs one of everything, every respect, every idea, every hope
        and every memory
And yet leaves sufficient wealth behind,
The courage to be in this certain-of-uncertainty world.

MAPPING

The path is any direction followed to the end
Because in every direction lie coiled difficulties
Enough to ensure the full engagement
Of the memory of the ideas of the world
The advantages of estimating advantage
The Chimeras and Hollywoods of montaged images
The spontaneous arisings of colors and visions
The certainty of this and this and this amortizing to that,
The eight-sided ship that navigates motion,
The tastes that arrange the eating of existence,
The two receptacles that pump in and out the fresh and stinking,
The two eavesdroppers that spy upon the conspiratorial hubbub,
The two conquerors of time and distance,
The tiger who kills and the pig who swines and swills,
The seven writhings of the worm,
And the swarm of thousands of little sticks puppeted about,
And when they are occupied in their tasks
At the life - or - death intensity level
I can escape to where they can never go
And climb the ladder that reaches to the Way
Wherein astonishments beckon
To the four infinities of Reality's evolution,
And on the two legs of the Wilderness Intellect
I can race those regions of pure delight-action,
Changing at the same time inner and outer direction
In Moment - of - Beauty after Moment - of - Beauty
Whose lightnings shake with their thunder
The icosahedron of fate.

The great lemnicate paths
Bulling through the gravitational fields
Washed by Radioactive Hurricanes from Supernova
Picking up a proton of mass
With ever nano-second's volume advance
Did not till yesterday

73

come to Homo Sapien's attention,
And only the day before did he learn
How Earth had traveled to make the fields
In which the Biosphere had evolved his recent presence,
That the atoms held the energy
to blow him and all his works away,
And he still does not realize
That all his states, dogmas, morals, and economics
Were concerted by terrified and plotting fantasies
The great imperatives emerge,
Dare to know
Dare to be
Dare to do
Dare to keep silent
Dare to abandon the nest which hatched the egg
Dare to soar and plummet
Dare to accomplish your life
Dare to not transmit your superstitions.

Other publications from Synergetic Press

FICTION
39 Blows On A Gone Trumpet
by Johnny Dolphin

Dolphin, the latest to emerge from the Tangier school of writing. Captivating prose that swings with its own rhythm, 39 riffs sounding unique historical beats of Manhattan, Iran, and Tangier. $5.95/£4.50

POETRY
On Feet of Gold
by Ira Cohen

Selected poetry. Catharsis and prophesy are combined through incisive and penetrating imagery of man as he is, in contrast to the poet's vision of man as he might be. $7.95/£5.75

DRAMA
The Collected Works of the Caravan of Dreams Theater: Volume I and II
by Johnny Dolphin

Volume I includes Caravan's adaptations/translations of three classic dramas, *Gilgamesh, Marouf the Cobbler*, and *Faust: Part One*; Volume II contains three original plays of modern times, *Billy the Kid, Metal Woman, Tin Can Man*. $5.95/£3.95

Kabuki Blues Comic
Conceived and Illustrated by Corinna MacNeice
Based on Caravan of Dreams Theater production.

Exciting new strokes in comic books. $1.50/£1.00

BIOSPHERICS
Space Biospheres
by John Allen and Mark Nelson

A compelling vision of a possible future which moves the dream of the space frontier from the realms of science fiction into the practical domain of science and management. $6.95/£4.95

The Biosphere Catalogue
Editor in Chief, T. P. Snyder
Scientific Editor, John Allen

A comprehensive presentation of the biosphere, with contributions from over thirty leading figures in fields ranging from atmosphere, hydrosphere, geosphere, plants and animals to cultures, cities, space biospheres, genetics and travel. $12.95/£9.95

The Biosphere
by V. I. Vernadsky
The first English edition of the classic work by Vernadsky originally published in Russian in 1926. $5.95/£3.95

Feng-Shui
by Ernest J. Eitel
with commentary by John Michell

The science of sacred landscape in old China. The first English treatise ever written on the Chinese code of practice used in overall matters of architectural design, city planning and use of the countryside. $5.95/£3.95

Succeed
A Handbook On Structuring Managerial Thought
by John Allen

A wholly new, philosophically profound and at the same time eminently practical analysis of the art and science of management. $8.00/£5.75